Auctioned To The Kodiak Shifter

Highest Bidder

Olivia T. Turner

Copyright© 2023 by Olivia T. Turner.
All rights reserved. No part of this book may be reproduced or transmitted in any form or by any means, electronic or mechanical, including emailing, photocopying, printing, recording, or by any information storage and retrieval system, without permission in writing from the author. For permission requests, email Olivia@oliviatturner.com

This is a work of fiction. Any resemblance to actual events, businesses, companies, locales or persons, living or dead, is entirely coincidental.
Contains explicit love scenes and adult language.
18+

www.OliviaTTurner.com

Edited by Karen Collins Editing

To Marie,
Who would auction herself off to a billionaire in a heartbeat,
if such a crazy thing exited.

Chapter One

Ava

Five years. I can't believe it's already been five whole years.

I stare at the crappy store-bought cupcake on the counter of the reception desk and sigh. It doesn't even look good. Just empty calories with no taste.

In a way, this cupcake is perfectly fitting to celebrate an anniversary of this mind-numbingly boring job—It offers no excitement and it will leave a bland taste in my mouth just like this place does to me every single day.

Five freaking years. The days go by so slow, but the years... they go by even slower.

I'm only twenty-five, but somedays I feel as old as Harold.

"Hi Harold," I say as he shuffles by with his nose in a dusty old tomb of a book. The binding is cracked, the pages are yellow, and it seems to be disintegrating before my very eyes.

He grumbles something and doesn't look up. This old weathered man, who is my only coworker by the way, barely ever says a word to me. And when he does, it's to ask if I've seen some rare obscure philosophical text by Confucius' barber or something similar.

That's life in *The Relic Repository*. We're a library in Seattle that specializes in old obscure ancient texts. We have rows upon dusty rows of religious texts, philosophical texts, historical texts, and old ancient literary texts. If it's old and boring, we have it. What we don't have are windows. Apparently, sunlight is one of the main enemies to these old brittle pages, so the only window—a tiny one along the right wall—is covered by an old painting of some wrinkly monk.

Sometimes when Harold is in the back, engrossed in a giant book about ancient Egyptian accounting practices or something equally boring and dull, I'll move the painting and stare into the alley for a few minutes.

I really wish it would open. I've gotten used to the stale musty smell in here, but sometimes it hits me out of the blue and I long desperately for some fresh air.

"Harold," I say as he continues shuffling past the reception. "Guess what?"

He sighs with annoyance as he tears his eyes off the old yellowed pages and turns to me. His brown eyes are small and beady behind his thick round glasses. His gray eyebrows are out of control as usual and he's wearing the same tweed jacket and brown tie that he's worn all week. At least, he's changed his shirt.

"I couldn't possibly guess what goes on in that feeble brain of yours," he says in a dry scratchy voice. His voice makes him sound like he's one hundred years old, but his appearance makes him look like he's one hundred and five.

"It's about the cupcake," I say with a grin. "Guess what today is."

"Your birthday."

"Nope."

He stands there staring at me like it's taking all of his energy and patience to tolerate my 'generation's dullness of intellect'—a favorite saying of his.

"It's my fifth anniversary of working here," I say with jazz hands. "Can you believe it?"

"Call me when you get to fifty years."

He turns back to the ancient volume in his hands and continues shuffling into the back.

I sigh as I stare at the cupcake. Is it too early to eat it? It's too early to eat it. This dull bland cupcake will be the excitement of my day and I want to make it last. It's only 9:16, so I have a long monotonous day ahead of me.

On a busy week, we'll get about eight people coming in here, mostly professors and scholars who find what they want on their own and quietly read in a corner or take a photo of the pages on their phones and then leave.

It's a dark dreary place with peeling paint and stained carpets that lost their color around the '70s from what I can tell. I thought this job would be exciting. I thought it would be an adventure.

I thought that thrilling characters like Indiana Jones and that guy from The Da Vinci Code would be bursting in here to look up some ancient texts to help on their next adventurous crusade. I thought they would take me along with them as their sexy/sassy love interest.

But alas, no. The only type of people coming in here are

like Mrs Tuffin, a quiet professor who reads through boring old religious texts while crunching on carrot sticks.

Fuck it.

I sigh as I grab my cupcake, sit back in my chair, open my romance novel, and get to work on another thrilling day as I take a big bite of the bland frosting. It's even worse than I thought it would be.

Five years...

I can't even focus on the words. I read the same sentence four times and I can't grasp any of it. With a sigh, I toss the book on the desk and stare at the yellow stains on the ceiling.

How the hell did I let my life become so... uninspiring?

When I was a kid, I had dreams of adventure, of travel, of having experiences worth writing in a book. I was convinced that I would have this epic love affair full of danger and excitement.

I'm twenty-five and I'm ashamed to say, I still haven't even had my first kiss.

There's been no great love affair, no travel, no adventure, no nothing. Just dusty old books and Harold's unamused frowns.

I polish off the cupcake, toss the wrapper into the garbage, and then immediately regret that I was so quick to eat it. What the hell am I going to look forward to now?

I don't even look forward to my shift ending anymore. Every evening is the same. I go back to my small apartment, cook a quick uninspiring dinner, eat it in front of whatever sitcom I'm watching on Netflix, and wait until it's 9:30 so I can go to bed.

Five years...

What, am I supposed to keep this up for another five? Then what? Another ten, twenty, fifty? Am I going to turn into Harold? Is anything ever going to change for me or is this it?

I drop my head back, close my eyes, and let out a loud groan of frustration.

"*Shhhhh!*" Harold admonishes from the back.

If something doesn't change, I'm going to lose my mind.

These are supposed to be my prime years. I'm supposed to be meeting exciting people and going out with friends. When I moved here from the small town I grew up in, I had visions of having a big hot boyfriend and laughing while hanging out with a big group of friends, but it's hard to make friends in the city, especially when you're as introverted as I am.

The front door opens and I perk up in my seat.

An older man walks in, brushing the light rain off his long coat. I recognize him as the dean of one of the nearby colleges. Apparently his family is very wealthy, but he's just so rude that I can't even.

He walks right up to me without making eye contact and pulls a thick book from the inside of his coat. With a scowl on his face, he drops the heavy book on the counter with a thud so loud it startles me.

"Thanks," I say flatly as he walks to the tall dusty bookshelves that stretch from the floor to the ceiling. *Jerk.*

Finally, something to do.

I slide the book off the counter and frown as I read the title. "Law Code of Hammurabi, 1754 BC. Wow, looks fascinating."

I roll my eyes as I turn to place it on the counter behind me. I'm excited to put it away, but it's going to be a long day, so I have to pace myself. I'll let myself re-shelve it in an hour. Not before.

As I place the book on the counter, a thick paper slides out and falls to the floor.

"What the fuck?" I whisper as I pick it up. "An auction... for women?"

What kind of weird shit is the dean into?

I hide it in a drawer until he leaves and then I whip it out with my heart pounding.

The Breeding Bidders Auction House.

My eyes dart around the invitation, reading it in record speed as my pulse races.

"You have been cordially invited to an exclusive auction reserved for the most elite billionaires on the planet."

Okay....

"We believe that you would enjoy this unique opportunity to participate in this extraordinary, unique, and rare event. This auction will feature an exquisite selection of handpicked *virgins*... What the fuck?!"

I lower the paper as I look around with my skin tingling and my nerves on edge. I'm alone in the room and the only sound is the soft rustling of pages as Harold flips through a book in his office.

With a deep breath, I turn back to the invitation.

"We are confident that you will find the girl of your dreams among the selection of beautiful willing maidens. The event will take place in Montana on the seventeenth of September in a private secluded area accessible by *private jet*."

I swallow hard as I lower the paper and stare forward in shock. The auction is four months away... I wonder if the dean is actually going to go.

"We are confident that you will find the selection of innocent young women on offer to be truly breathtaking and that you will be thrilled to have the opportunity to bid on them.

"Please RSVP at your earliest convenience to secure your place at this exclusive auction. We look forward to hearing from you soon. Yours truly, Coco St. James."

My heart is racing as I stare at the phone number discreetly printed under the unusual name and then at the six photos of girls printed at the bottom.

Willing young virgins... Where do they get these women?

They all seem to be in their early to mid twenties. All beautiful, but with a girl next door kind of look to them.

I stare at them for a long while, imagining the billionaires looking at them and wanting them to be their brides so badly they'd bid millions of dollars.

Now that would be an adventure. Marrying a billionaire and traveling around the world. Seeing the planet and meeting interesting people.

Wow...

I slip the invitation into the drawer, shake my head, and try to continue reading my book, but I quickly find that thinking about anything but that auction is impossible.

For the rest of the morning, I keep pulling it out, staring at the girls, and picturing my photo there. Would anyone bid on me?

I keep dreaming about a gorgeous man charging forward, not letting anyone outbid him for the pleasure of having me as his wife because with one look, he was obsessed.

He would whisk me off into his exciting world and I wouldn't care about the money because I'd be falling in love with that beautiful smile and the possessive way he looks at me.

We could start a family, have children, spend the rest of our thrilling lives in one adventure after another.

I trace my tingling fingertip over the embossed phone number as Harold shuffles back into the room, holding his lunch in a brown paper bag.

"What's for lunch, Harold?" I ask even though he's had the same tuna on white bread, no crusts, and four Ritz crackers for the past five years.

"Tuna on white bread, no crusts, with four Ritz crackers."

He shuffles past me without asking what I'm having.

I sigh as I stare at the number.

"Screw it," I whisper. I dial the number and then suck in a breath. My heart races as it rings.

"The Breeding Bidders Auction House," a woman on the other line says. *"How may I help you?"*

I open my mouth as I stare at the desk with wide eyes. Nothing comes out.

"Hello? How did you get this number?"

"From a friend!" I blurt out.

"And what is it concerning?"

I take a deep breath as I stare forward, wondering if I should take the plunge. If I should throw caution to the wind and turn my life upside down.

I have to make a change sometime. It's never going to feel like it's the right time. It's never going to feel easy.

Sometimes in life, you have to play the cards you're delt, but sometimes you have to flip the damn table over to shake things up.

"Miss, what is this concerning?"

"The auction!" I say with adrenaline rushing through my veins. "I'd like to be auctioned off!"

Chapter Two

Elias

I storm over to Novak's trailer with an unstoppable rage ripping through my tense body. I've had enough of this motherfucker.

He's been pushing my buttons all goddamn summer, buying up all the forested land around my ranch and polluting the shit out of it with his fracking company.

I've been wanting to let my Kodiak maul this bastard, but I've always held the furry beast back. Until now.

This morning, when my bear was roaming through the forest on *my* land that *my* father owned and *my* grandfather before him, I found a team of engineers planning where they're going to start drilling.

I nearly lost it. I scared them pretty good with my bear though. They won't be back for a while.

This billionaire asshole thinks he can do whatever he wants because he's willing to throw around some cash.

Well, my land is *not* for sale. It's staying in my family and if I'm lucky enough to find my mate and have some cubs one day, I'll hand it over to them when the time comes, and I'll make damn sure the property is in *pristine* shape.

"*Novak*," I roar as I yank open the flimsy door. I march into his trailer and find him sitting behind his desk.

"Mr. Gatlin," he says with a grin on his face. "Have you come to make a deal?"

Even my Kodiak bear hates this guy. He's pacing around angrily inside, snarling and snapping his big jaws at the rank smell of cigar that's always following this asshole around. He's an old, out of shape man at around sixty five years if I had to guess. Barely a hint of hair on his bald head and several thick rolls of skin on the back of his neck. A small pair of glasses are perched on his big bulbous nose.

This town—Clarington Springs—was such a beautiful place before he moved in with his huge machinery that I can hear roaring all the way to my ranch. He's cut down thousands of trees, ripped up the beautiful land, and polluted at least two rivers.

"I'll make a deal with you," I say through gritted teeth as I march over and slam my fists on his desk. The cheap wood groans under my knuckles. He leans back in his chair with a cocky smile as I lean forward.

I could snap this guy in half. He's zero match for me physically, but he's still got that arrogant way about him that only a billionaire can have. Unfortunately, money means power and he's got an inexhaustible supply of it.

But he better not push me too far. Money isn't the only type of power and I got the other kind in spades. I'm a shifter hiding a vicious Kodiak bear inside my body and he's extra cranky since I'm forty-five years old and we still haven't even had a whiff of our mate yet.

"The deal is," I say with a growl. "You stay off my property and you can keep your fucking head. Send your goons onto my land one more time and I'll tear your fucking throat out. Got it?"

He sneers as he picks up an unlit cigar and runs it through his fingers. "That wasn't the deal proposed, Mr. Gatlin," he says as he runs the cigar under his nose, inhaling the rich tobacco. "Seven million for your ranch."

"Get fucked."

"Since I'm in such a generous mood," he says with a grin. "I'll increase the offer to eight million. Now, that's two million above market value."

"It's not for sale," I roar. "It will *never* be for sale. Who the fuck do you think you are? You've ruined this town!"

"I brought investment to this town," he says as he explodes out of his chair with a nasty look on his face. "My workers are pouring money into this shit hole area. Ask the restaurants and bars how much they like having me here with my workers filling their tables *and* their cash registers."

"You're destroying the land," I say as my blood boils. "Who cares about full tables in a restaurant if you've clear-cut all the trees off the goddamn mountain and polluted the fucking rivers? You've ruined this area for a generation!"

"I'm creating energy for millions," he snaps back. "Providing the population with necessary wood and minerals. Where do you think the shit packing department stores' shelves come from? The moon? Don't be naive."

I want to squeeze his neck until those vile eyes close for good. My muscles are all tense and twitchy, begging me for it.

"This place was a paradise until you and your—"

All of the violent energy and intense rage ripping

through me vanishes in an instant when I see the paper on his desk.

I freeze, stunned to the core as I stare at one of the photos printed at the bottom. My heart pounds so hard I can feel it in my ears.

"*What...*"

I feel numb all over as I slowly pick up the thick paper, turn it around, and look at the beautiful face smiling shyly at me.

It's her...

How can it be her? What is this? Why is she on here?

My bear lets out a low growl as I stare at the stunning blue eyes looking back at me. This is my mate. I'm looking at my mate.

A knot settles in my stomach as my mind begins to swirl. I've never seen her before, but there's no doubt in mind that I'm looking at her right now. Every cell in my body has come alive.

Even my bear is reacting, pacing around and letting me know he wants me to get her.

"What is this?" I ask as I try to focus on the words. "An auction for women?"

My mate is being auctioned off?

I whip my head up and glare at Novak. "What. Is. This?"

"Someone on there catch your eye?" he asks with a grin.

"What the fuck is this? Where is she?"

He smiles like he's got me. "That there is the most exclusive auction on the planet. Billionaires from all over the world come together for The Breeding Bidders Auction House to outbid each other for the pleasure of wedding beautiful young virgins."

I look at her photo and feel like I'm going to be sick. I

can't let my mate be auctioned off to a creep like Novak.

I spot the date on the bottom. It's in the town next to ours in two days.

"How can I get in there?" I ask as I squeeze the paper in my fist. "I *need* this girl."

He waddles over to his desk chair and casually sits down, playing with his unlit cigar. I want to slap the smug look off his face, but he might be the only one who can get me in the same room as my mate.

"I'm afraid it's for billionaires only," he says with a sad sarcastic shake of his head. "Not for blue collar workers like you."

"Don't play with me, Novak," I growl. "This is my mate."

His face lights up, but he quickly hides it. "Mate or not, these girls are auctioned off for *millions* of dollars. Do you have that kind of money, Elias?"

An overwhelming sense of dread takes over my body. I feel dizzy. I need some air.

"You'll have a better chance of securing your mate," he says as he runs the cigar through his fingers, "*if* you have seven million dollars in your hand."

I grit my teeth as I glare at him. "You said eight million."

"That was before," he says with a grin. "The offer is now back to seven."

My whole body flexes tight as I glare at him. I can't sell my ranch. But I can't let my mate go either.

"Seven and a half," I growl.

He leaps up from his chair and shakes my hand. "Deal. I'll have my attorneys handle the paperwork and you'll have your money before the auction starts."

My head is spinning as he sits back down and lights his cigar in triumph.

I'm going to lose my land... The land my grandfather settled and my father grew up on. The land I adore and hoped to leave to my children one day.

But it doesn't matter. My mate is all that matters.

I won't have any children to pass on my legacy to without her anyway.

My father would understand. My grandfather too. They were both Kodiak bear shifters as well and would have done anything for their mates.

I don't need my ranch if I have her. Hell, I'd live in an abandoned haunted house if it meant being able to wrap my protective arms around her every night.

I stare at the picture as thick cigar smoke billows into the air.

"You can keep that," Novak says as he ashes into the huge crystal ashtray on his desk. "And good luck at the auction. I hope nobody outbids you."

My stomach drops as I fold the paper, being careful not to crease her picture, and stuff it into my back pocket.

"Now go pack your shit," he says with a sneer. "I want you out of that house and off my land before the first little slut struts onto that auction stage."

My bear snarls as I squeeze my hand into a fist, wanting to slam it into his fucking face. But I need that money more than I need to teach this piece of shit a lesson.

With a huff of breath, I turn and storm out of the trailer, slamming the door as I leave.

When the fresh mountain air hits me, I take a deep breath and look at the photo one more time.

She's incredible. She'll soon be mine.

I don't know where in the world she is, but she'll be in my arms soon.

And nothing else will matter.

Chapter Three

Ava

"Are you nervous?" the red headed girl sitting at the vanity next to mine asks. I'm touching up my makeup, but I'm not sure why. The professional makeup artists did an amazing job. So did the hair stylist. I've never looked so beautiful. I didn't even realize I could look like this.

"Yeah," I say as my stomach flips and turns. "This felt like a good idea at the time, but now..."

"I know, right?" she says. "I was thinking that a handsome European prince would bid on me, but now I'm worried about some weirdo creep who still can't get laid even though he's a billionaire getting his grubby hands on me." She shivers at the thought. "My mother always says that I see life through rose-colored glasses. She also says that I watch too many Disney movies."

I smile as I look at her. She's gorgeous. She'll probably have the highest bids out of all of us.

"I'm doing this for her," she says as she gets a little misty eyed. "She has cancer and the bills are getting out of control. I already sent her the money we got."

"I'm sorry," I say as we share a moment. "What's your name?"

"Trinity, and you?"

"Ava."

"Let's hope there's enough hot rich princes in the audience for all of us," she says with a smile. I feel a little better now. Less alone.

It's been a hell of a terrifying ride so far. If this is what adventure is then give me back my safe little boring life at the library. I don't think I'm made for this much uncertainty.

The auction house flew me out to Manhattan for a few days where they put me up in a gorgeous hotel suite near Times Square. I had a photoshoot for the invitation, which was a blast and then I got paid. One million dollars.

It's just sitting in my bank account and I have no idea what to do with it.

All I've done so far is open it every now and then and stare at the big number in awe.

"I love your dress," Trinity says as she looks me over.

"Oh, thanks," I say, feeling beautiful yet ridiculous at the same time. It's a huge pink evening gown that drags along the ground behind me. It's a stunning dress, but wildly impractical. I need a team of assistants following me around to lift it over objects and carry it up stairs. "You look great too."

She smiles as she looks at the white gown she's wearing. "Do you think we'll be wearing gowns like this and going to huge galas full of interesting people in our new lives? I can just imagine walking into a huge glamorous hall on the arm of my prince as foreign dignitaries come over and kiss my hand."

I'm trying not to twist my face up in disgust as I stare at her. That may be good for her, but I would *hate* that. I'm an introvert and big parties full of strangers I have to talk to all night are not my thing. I would prefer a man who likes to stay home most nights. Someone big and warm that I can curl up to with a good book.

Oh no. I didn't even think of that. What if I get someone who's dragging me to all sorts of corporate parties and fancy balls? I'd die.

A heavy feeling sinks into my body as I start to panic. This was a bad idea. I don't want to be here.

"Are you okay?" Trinity asks as she looks at me.

Why did I do this? What the hell is the matter with me? An auction for billionaires? I was too afraid to make a Tinder profile and now I'm about to walk on stage in front of a room full of mysterious rich men from all over the planet who are going to bid on me? And I have to marry the winner? Without even knowing his name?! I can't! I won't!

"Ava, what's wrong?" Trinity says as I dart up from my seat and head to the exit with my cheeks burning.

Coco St. James, the mean owner of the auction, steps in front of my path with a steely look. She's terrifying with her blonde bob and icy blue eyes.

"Where do you think you're going?" she snaps in her checkered power suit. If the devil came to earth, it would take a form similar to Coco.

"I was just... um, getting some air."

"No leaving," she says, her flinty voice like daggers. "The auction is about to start."

"Well, um... about that..." I'm twisting my fingers while trying to look in her eyes, but it's damn near impossible. She's too intimidating. "I think I've changed my mind."

She stares me down.

"I can give the money back."

"You signed a contract."

"I know, and I'm really sorry about that. I just don't think this is the right move for me."

"The right move?"

"Yeah, exactly. I'll give you back the dress, it's beautiful by the way, and then if someone can give me a ride to the airport, I'll find my own way home."

The corner of her lip curls up like she's amused.

"That's not how this works," she says in a low rigid voice. "You signed the contract, you took the money, and now there are a room full of billionaires eager to pay a high price for the honor of having you slip into their bed. There's no changing minds or second thoughts. Now, take your place and when it's your time to walk onto the stage, I better see happy smiles or you'll have a lot more to worry about than a bad first date with your new husband. Magnus! Door!"

My stomach sinks as she marches off. A huge imposing guard hurries over and stands in front of the door with his muscular arms crossed. He stares me down as a feeling of hopeless inevitability sets in.

There's nothing else I can do but go along with it. One of the workers wearing a headset microphone lines us up at the entrance to the stage. She quickly walks down the line, touching up makeup, fixing hair, and adjusting dresses. I notice that she doesn't look anyone in the eyes. We're all products to her. One more object to bid off.

"Remember to smile," she warns us as she fixes Trinity's hair. "Coco does not react well to girls who don't smile."

Smiling seems impossible right now. I'm trying really hard not to cry.

"Walk onto the stage, step on the little X taped there, and look as innocent and fuckable as possible." She pauses as someone says something into her earpiece. "Got it. First girl coming out in thirty seconds."

The excitement and nerves rippling down the line-up of girls gives me goosebumps.

"Good luck," Trinity says as she turns around with a big smile.

How can she be smiling? Wow, she really does go through life with rose-colored glasses on. I envy her.

"Get ready," the worker whispers with her hand on the door.

She gets the cue through her earpiece, pushes the door open, and the auction starts.

Chapter Four

Elias

This is so fucked up.

I'm sitting in a *huge* tent on some Montana ranch waiting for my girl to come out. Anonymity is key with a group like this, so the entire area is cloaked in darkness. The only bright area is the lit up stage that all the chairs are facing.

My pulse is racing as I wait for the auction to start. I have a million thoughts and emotions racing through me right now. I'm excited to finally meet my girl after decades of dreaming about her but I'm terrified that I might lose her to another bidder.

The big black duffel bag full of cash is between my feet. I signed the deal with Novak about two hours ago. He kept his word and I got seven and a half million dollars in stacks of cash. It cost me everything, even my truck since it was registered under the ranch. I had to hitchhike here, but I'd give up everything for my girl. All I need is her.

I don't know where we're going to live or what we're going to do, but we'll figure it out. Hopefully, I'll have some money left over that will allow us to start over somewhere new.

My bear grumbles with excitement as I picture us in a little house somewhere quiet. I can finally be at peace, knowing my mate is safe and secure in the same room as me. I smile as I picture her laughing at something I said, my heart so full of love it feels like it's going to burst.

A severe-looking lady marches onto the stage in a checkered pantsuit and walks over to the podium. I sit up straight in my seat as a murmur of excitement ripples through the dark crowd.

"Good evening," she says into the microphone as her sharp blue eyes scan the room. "And welcome to The Breeding Bidders Auction House. I am Coco St. James, the owner, operator, and auctioneer for tonight. All of the stunning young women you will be seeing this evening are here voluntarily. They are all verified virgins and each one is available to the highest bidder. If you are lucky enough to place the winning bid, payment will be due immediately. Upon payment received, you will be married on the spot to the gorgeous young virgin you have chosen."

A green button lights up on the armrest beside me. I see several of them lighting up all around the room.

"The Breeding Bidders Auction House has been operating for thirty-five years, proudly serving the ultra-wealthy in sixty-two countries. We understand that your time is extremely valuable, so we will begin without further delay. Our first lovely young virgin up for auction is Grace Walters, twenty-three years old."

A young blonde walks onto the stage looking nervous and a little freaked out as Coco St. James talks her up. "Miss Walters is item number one in our auction tonight. A creative soul with a wonderful singing voice, notice the square shoulders and light blue eyes."

Grace gets auctioned off to an older man who I kind of recognize. I think he's a tech guru or something.

My patience starts to fray as one girl after another gets paraded out and auctioned off. Most go for under five million dollars, but one goes for nine. That makes me nervous. I only have seven and a half.

Where is she?

I'm dying here.

A red headed girl named Trinity comes out and there's a fierce bidding war for her. A handsome young man who looks like he's a prince from some European country the way he's dressed gets the final bid in and wins. They both look ecstatic as Coco St. James marries them on the spot.

"Item number twelve of the evening," Coco goes on. "Ava Lennon. Twenty-five years old."

My mate steps onto the stage and my whole body stiffens. I stare at her, stunned as she walks onto the middle of the stage, looking radiant in a long pink gown.

Her long brown hair is pulled back and flowing out in exquisite waves. My blood is on fire as I stare at her in awe. When I picture taking the pins out of her hair and letting those silky locks fall loose on her bare shoulders, I have to hold onto the armrests of my chair to stop myself from running up to the stage and grabbing her.

She forces out a smile and even though I can tell she's nervous, it still makes my heart ache. My bear growls from inside. He hates this even more than I do.

All these predatory eyes leering at what's ours. My

hands squeeze into fists as I look around the dark room with my jaw clenched.

She's mine, I nearly roar out in warning.

"Notice the child-bearing hips on Miss Lennon," Coco says as my girl stands on the middle of the stage, so exposed, so vulnerable.

A fierce protective side I didn't know I had makes itself known. I cling to my seat as my body screams at me to go hide her from all these eyes.

"We'll start the bidding at one million dollars," Coco says. "Do I have one million?"

I'm so shaken that I don't get the first bid out.

Someone hits the green button on their seat before I do. I want to tear his fucking throat out for that.

"Do we have one point five million?"

I slam my fist on the green button before anyone else can.

"One point five. Do we have two million?"

That same fucker bids again. My bear snarls in fury.

I slam my button when she says three, but that fucker keeps outbidding me.

My anger turns to panic when the bidding passes seven million. I only have seven and a half and I can't lose her.

"Seven," I cry out as I hit the green button.

"We have seven," Coco echoes. "Do we have seven point five?"

My hands are trembling as I look at the area where the other bidder is sitting. He stays quiet. He's not bidding any higher!

She's mine! I'll finally have my mate by my side. I'm forty-five years old and I've been dreaming of this moment since puberty. It's finally here. Ava will finally be with me where she belongs.

Tears of happiness and gratitude flood my eyes as Coco counts down.

"Last chance," she says as she holds the gavel up. "Seven million going once, going twice—"

"Eight million," a familiar voice shouts out from behind me.

I yank my head around in shock and fury in the direction of the voice. My eyes focus through the darkness—my shifter vision allowing me to see who I really don't want to be seeing right now. I grit my teeth in rage when I spot Troy Novak grinning in triumph.

That fucker... He planned this all along.

He's got my ranch and now he's about to get my girl.

"Eight million," Coco says as my stomach drops and my bear whimpers. "Going once, going twice, sold to the gentleman in the back."

I feel like I'm going to be sick.

Novak stands up, straightens his suit jacket, and waddles over to the stage with four huge bodyguards following him. Who the hell are those guys? I can smell whiffs of grizzly bears coming from them.

He knew I was going to be furious, so he hired some shifter bodyguards to accompany him.

The way I'm feeling right now, I could charge through a hundred shifters to get to what's mine.

I stand up as he walks onto the stage. His bodyguards stand with their backs to him, ready to stop anyone from trying to get up the stairs.

My girl looks horrified as he grabs her hand and pulls her over to Coco.

"*No!*" I roar as I leap up from my seat and lunge forward. I leave the money and sprint down the aisle, ready to take off the head of anyone foolish enough to try and stop me.

Ava's beautiful blue eyes snap to mine and it drives me forward. My bear is desperate to come out, but I want to handle this on my own.

The guards get ready as I approach. Yup, they're all definitely grizzly bear shifters. I can smell them clearly now.

I throw two of them to the side, but the other two each grab an arm. I toss one off, but the other two leap onto my back.

They swarm me. Coco's lion shifter guards leap onto the pile and pretty soon, I'm bring dragged out by seven huge shifters.

I roar in outrage as the image of my mate gets smaller and smaller while I'm being dragged to the door.

They launch me outside and I land on my back with a grunt. One of the guards tosses my bag of money beside me and then closes the door and locks it.

I leap to my feet with my mind racing.

My mate is marrying my worst enemy.

And there's nothing I can do to stop it.

Chapter Five

Ava

Before this whole auction ordeal, the worst idea I ever had was trying to steal a box of lip gloss from the store where my aunt worked. My best friend at the time had pressured me into doing it even though I hated lip gloss.

I successfully slipped it into my bag while my friend was on the lookout, but as soon as my aunt saw my burning red cheeks, it was over. It was a whole thing. *Everyone* found out about it. I was humiliated.

Well, that's a distant second now compared to the mess I'm in at the moment.

"And do you, Ava Lennon, take this man to be your husband?" Coco St. James asks as she stares me down with those intense light blue eyes.

I cringe as Troy Novak reaches out and takes my hand. His skin feels like alligator scales. I hate it.

This is the guy who bid on me? *This* is the guy I have to marry?

What happened to the gorgeous guy they dragged out of here? Why couldn't he have been the one?

I want to scream and run out of here, but those guards are blocking the stairs. I wouldn't be surprised if Coco shot laser beams out of her eyes if I say no. She's terrifying.

She clears her throat and I squeak out a 'yes.'

"I now pronounce you husband and wife."

My stomach drops. I nearly bend over and retch. This can't be happening. This can't be my life now.

What was I *thinking*?

I wanted adventure? Since when does adventure ever end well for anyone?

Maybe there's a happy ending in movies and in romance books, but real life is always so different. There's never a hot guy at the end of it, carrying you into the sunset. In real life, you end up with a weird old man like this guy who kind of looks like the Penguin from some old Batman movie.

As I'm being dragged to the exit by my charming new husband, my mind keeps going back to the man who was roaring in agony as he was thrown out. Who was that guy?

The way his warm hazel eyes felt when they were on me... It felt like the wrong man won the auction. It felt like I belonged to him. That possessive look in his eyes made me feel like I was a part of his territory. Like I was his.

"Where are we going?" I ask as Troy grabs my wrist too hard. It hurts and I try to yank my arm away, but he's got an iron grip on it.

"I'm taking you home," he says in a chilling voice that gives me shivers.

His four enormous guards surround us as he pulls me outside through a back door in the large tent.

I can't go with him. If he takes me away from here, I might never be seen again. I might never get out of his clutches.

He pulls out his phone and I glance at the screen, watching as he texts someone named Sylvio to start the helicopter.

We step outside into the dark night and the cool air hits my face. I was enchanted with the gorgeous Montana mountains and the stunning scenery when we were driving in, but now, surrounded by dark wilderness, I'm scared of all the deadly creatures that may be lurking about.

I should be more scared of the dangerous creature clutching my wrist right now. This dangerous creature who is now my husband.

A helicopter at the end of a row of private jets lights up. The huge rotary blade begins to spin as I'm pulled toward it. It roars so loud that the tiny hairs on the back of my neck rise.

Only... the sound is coming from behind me.

We all turn around with a gasp as a huge bear comes charging out of the darkness, thundering forward on massive paws. Its lip is curled up in a snarl over long gleaming white teeth and its eyes... *No way...* It has the same possessive hazel eyes as the man in the auction. I'd recognize them anywhere. My whole body reacts to them in the same way it did before—erupting in tingles as I'm drawn to that protective stare.

Troy Novak turns to two of the guards. "Kane. Marcus. The one who brings me the severed head of that Kodiak bear gets paid double. I want to hang it over my fireplace."

I gasp as the two men explode into roaring grizzly bears. "What the fuck?!"

They're shifters?!

My new husband and the other two guards continue pulling me toward the helicopter as I look over my shoulder, desperately hoping that the Kodiak bear will be okay.

He charges into the two grizzly bears, colliding into them with his massive shoulders and sending them flying to the side. They don't stay down easily though. I suck in a breath when they get to their paws and chase after him.

The smallest of the bears is the fastest. He leaps onto the Kodiak bear's back and that allows the other to catch up. It's a blur of brown fur as the snarling bears brawl it out.

"Stop stalling!" Troy snaps as he squeezes my wrist harder and yanks me forward.

When we arrive at the helicopter, the Kodiak bear launches the two bears off with a furious growl and charges forward. He never takes his eyes off me. He looks like he's coming to save me, although with my luck, he's probably starving and has his sights on the tasty girl in the cotton candy-looking dress.

Still, I'll take my chances with the angry bear over Troy Novak any day.

One of the guards opens the door of the helicopter and waves us in. I can't get in there. I plant my heels into the ground and slam my elbow into my new husband's ribs.

"You *bitch*," he roars as he grabs me by the back of the neck and tries to force me into the chopper. I grab onto the sides of the door and hold on. "You two! Stop that fucking bear!"

The two remaining guards yank off their shirts and then run toward the charging Kodiak bear. They each burst into grizzly bears mid-stride as I fight with Troy who's still trying to get me into the helicopter.

I kick him in the shins and elbow him in the neck as the blood-curdling sound of bears fighting hits my ears. The growling and snarling quickly turn to whimpers.

"*Novak!*" a deep booming voice shouts from behind us. "Get your fucking hands off my mate."

We both turn around with a gasp. The man from the auction is standing there in the nude, watching us with a fire in his eyes as he storms over.

The four guards are behind him, all back in their human forms, all writhing on the ground in agony.

There's a long bloody gash on the man's shoulder, but he doesn't even seem to notice. All of his attention and focus is on us.

Novak grabs my arm and pulls a gun from inside his jacket. He points it at the man's chest.

The man shakes his head as he calmly walks forward. "You think a bullet will stop me?"

"No," Novak says as he turns the gun and digs it into my ribs. "But it will stop her. Now get back or I'll put a bullet in her."

The four naked guards make their way over, groaning in pain as they stand beside us. They're all breathing heavily as they face the man.

"We had a deal, Novak," the man roars over the sound of the chopper.

"The deal was for your ranch, Elias. Nothing was said about your mate."

"I didn't think I had to make a deal about that," Elias shouts. "I didn't think you were stupid enough to come between a bear shifter and his girl."

"She's my girl now," Novak yells with a nasty grin.

"Bought and paid for. Now, kindly fuck off. I'd like to start my honeymoon."

He pulls me into the helicopter with the help of his goons and the man watches helplessly as Novak holds the gun to my head.

The ground jerks under us as the helicopter rises into the air. One of the guards slams the door closed, and gun on me or not, I have to get one last look at him.

I lunge forward and plaster my hands on the window as I look down at the beautiful man with my heart breaking.

He's staring up at me with agony in his eyes.

Elias is the man who should have won.

He's the one I want.

We rise into the sky, and just before turning the chopper to the side, I see Elias change into his Kodiak bear and start sprinting.

Chapter Six

Elias

For over an hour, my bear sprints all-out through the mountains, desperate to get to our mate before Novak can put his sleazy hands on her.

Come on, I say, urging him on. *She needs us.*

The poor beast is running on empty, but he keeps going, sprinting as fast as he can to get to Novak's mansion at the base of Blackened Peak Mountain.

It's up ahead, I tell him when I see it in the light of the full moon. *You're almost there.*

By the time we arrive, he's exhausted. The Kodiak can barely lift its head anymore. It took every last ounce of his strength to get us here and now, I'll do the rest.

I pull him in and burst out with my heart pounding. We share some energy and I'm feeling more drained than I did before, but I get a boost of adrenaline when I see Novak's helicopter parked on the roof of his mansion.

Remembering the sight of my sweet Ava in the window looking down at me with those sad pleading eyes fires me up once again. I grit my teeth and sneak over to the back door, being careful to stay downwind since I know the four guards are probably still lurking around.

I break the door open with my shoulder and sneak inside, trying to stay as quiet as I can. The door leads to the home gym where I spot a pair of workout shorts folded on a shelf. I quickly slip them on.

I head deeper into the house, sneaking through the dark bar area when I hear Novak's voice coming from upstairs. The thought of him up there with my girl makes me snap. I run through the house, flying up stairs and barreling around corners as adrenaline surges through my veins.

I catch her scent in the upstairs hallway and it's like fire blazing down my throat and into my lungs. This time, my Kodiak bear urges me on, snarling and gnashing his teeth with every step I get closer.

Her sweet fiery scent leads to the huge double doors at the end of the hallway. I charge down it at full speed and slam my shoulder into where the doors connect. They explode open and I let out a low territorial growl at what I see.

My girl is tied to the bed—still in that pink dress—as Troy Novak spins around in shock.

His jacket is off, his tie loose, and from the stunned expression on his face, I can tell he wasn't expecting to see me again.

He lunges for the pistol on the dresser, but I'm faster. I grab his arm and snap it in the wrong direction.

"*Fuck!*" he screams in agony as I grab him by the neck and carry him to the balcony.

"She's mine," he hisses through gritted teeth. "I paid for her fair and square. You just can't handle losing!"

I squeeze his neck a little harder and his eyes bulge.

"You took the game too far, Novak," I growl as we pass through the French doors and onto the balcony. "Taking a bear's mate will always end up in a checkmate."

He claws at my wrist, trying to say something. His feet are off the ground and he's kicking my legs, desperately trying to wiggle free. I loosen my grip so he can speak.

"What?"

"I have money!" he hisses. "I'll pay you!"

"It's always money with you," I say as I shake my head. "Your money has saved you for the last time."

With a grunt, I launch him off the balcony. He screams the whole way down and then dies with a splat.

I look over the edge to make sure he's dead.

My Kodiak grumbles with satisfaction when he sees the puddle of blood leaking out of his cracked skull.

There's no guilt or sadness when I see his dead body, only relief. All threats to my mate must be ruthlessly eliminated. There's no other option. When it comes to keeping my Ava safe, there's nothing I won't do.

His four goons come running out of the darkness and surround Novak's dead body. They look stunned as they stand there staring down at their former boss.

"Up there!" one of them shouts when he sees me.

Shit!

I dart back inside as they hurry into the mansion.

The beautiful sight of my girl on the bed staggers me for a second, but I fight through it and race over.

"You came back for me," she whispers as I untie the string around her wrist.

Her blue eyes are so magnificent. I just want to stare at her for hours, admiring every stunning detail but those fuckers are on their way up and we have to move fast.

"Of course, I did," I say as I free one hand and then get to work on the other. "You're my girl, Ava. I'll die to keep you safe."

I get her second hand free and she grabs the back of my neck and pulls me toward her, crushing her lips to mine. My whole body goes numb when I taste her sweet mouth.

It's torture to pull away, but those goons are on their way up.

I pull my mouth away from hers with my head spinning. "We have to move. Now."

She leaps off the bed, but it's hard for her to move with that long train on her dress dragging behind her.

"Hold on," I say as I grab the thick fabric at her knees and tear it off.

I look at her, expecting her to be upset that I ruined her gorgeous gown, but she's got wide excited eyes and a fiery smile on her face.

"We're going to have to jump off the balcony," I tell her. "Are you ready for that?"

"Wait!" She runs over to the desk and grabs the gun and a stack of papers. "The marriage certificate. I didn't want to marry him. I was hoping you'd win."

She tosses the stack of papers into the fire and they light up with a roar.

I spot the file full of all the contracts I signed this afternoon that give Novak the deed to my ranch, so I grab them off the desk and toss them in as well.

"I will win," I say as I wrap my arm around her waist and pull her against me. I kiss her soft lips and then scoop her up into my arms as the papers burn. "And you'll be my wife."

The grizzly bear shifters are thumping up the stairs, so I run to the balcony with Ava clutched to my chest.

I hold her as tightly as I can and leap off.

Chapter Seven

Ava

"Holy shit!" I scream as Elias leaps off the balcony with me in his arms. I curl into his big warm chest as my stomach drops.

We hit the ground hard, but Elias absorbs all of the shock. He lands on his feet and starts running into the forest.

I peek over his big round shoulder and see the four bear shifters running onto the porch. They look at us fleeing and then leap over as well. I duck down with a whimper.

There's a gun in my hand, this huge shirtless beast of a man is holding me to his naked chest as he runs through the forest, and four vicious bear shifters are chasing us down with the intent to kill. I wanted adventure and now I got it.

I'm kind of changing my mind on the whole adventure thing. It's *terrifying*. I think the biggest adventure I can handle is maybe slipping a lemon slice into my tea for a change and switching up my book genre from romance to thriller.

"Are you okay?" Elias asks in his deep sexy voice. His big arms are cradled around me as those muscular legs sprint through the forest.

"I'm great!" I answer, not knowing what else to say. "Thanks. And you?"

"You're here with me," he says as he looks down at me like I'm the most precious thing he's ever seen. "That's all that matters."

I peek over that big shoulder again and gasp when I see two grizzly bears chasing us. Elias has got a big lead on them, but he's also carrying me, which has to slow him down. I'd run on my own, but they'd catch me in about three seconds flat. I'm not very fast in the best conditions and running through the forest at night would make me as fast as a sleepy turtle.

The roaring of engines hits my ears. "What is that?"

Two spotlights cut through the dark forest and I duck back down when I realize that two of them are on dirt bikes. This is getting worse and worse. We have two rabid grizzly bears chasing us and two deadly men on dirt bikes.

I have to do something! I can't just lay here in Elias' big comforting arms.

My eyes drop to the gun in my hand. I reach over Elias' shoulder and point the gun at one of the spotlights.

I'm bouncing around so much that it's hard to aim. Just as I pull the trigger, Elias leaps over a rock and the gun flies up. I put two bullets into the top of a tree.

"Shit!" I screech. "Sorry, tree!"

One of the dirt bikes is the first to catch up.

"Hold on!" Elias shouts as he shoves me onto his left shoulder while running. I'm bouncing around with one hand on his muscular back and the other clutching the gun, trying not to slip off as the dirt bike roars up on Elias' right side.

Elias swings his arm out, punching the guy in the face with the back of his fist as the dirt bike speeds up. He punches him so hard that I can feel the thumping crack in my body. The dirt bike swerves to the right and slams into a tree with so much force the whole thing comes tumbling down.

I scream as I cling to Elias' back. The thick tree trunk crashes into the ground, blocking the path of the two bears and the other dirt bike.

"I think we lost them!" I shout in triumph, and a little too early.

The two grizzlies leap over the fallen tree, followed by the roaring dirt bike.

"Nope!" I scream. "Scratch that! They're still following us."

"Shoot them, my love."

"I tried to but I hit a tree!"

"I know you can do it," Elias says in an encouraging tone as he races through the dark forest. "I'd do it myself, but they'll catch up."

I lift my shaking hand and point the gun at the bigger and scarier of the two bears.

With my heart pounding and adrenaline whipping through my veins, I pull the trigger twice. I think I hit the bear's leg because he collapses as he runs, summersaulting forward before he slams into a tree so hard all of the branches shake.

"I shot one of the bears!" I say as he carries me deeper into the forest. "I didn't like it at all!"

"I'm sorry, my mate. He'll be fine. He'll heal quickly,

but it will be enough to slow him down and keep him off our tail. You did so great!"

"Why do you keep calling me your mate?" I ask when it finally clicks. Is this big hulking bear shifter my mate?

The other dirt bike arrives before he can answer.

"Cling to my back," Elias shouts as he tries to outrun it.

"What?!"

He slings me over his back and I wrap my arms and legs around him like a baby koala. The shifter pulls ahead, skids the dirt bike to a stop, and then leaps off with his fists up.

He looks so scary and intimidating with his shaved head, muscular frame, and crazy eyes.

Elias doesn't even break stride. He runs right up to him and tries to punch him, but the grizzly shifter ducks out of the way of his fist. We slow to a stop as the two men face each other with their fists up.

I'm still clinging to his back, too terrified to let go.

Elias hits him with two jabs, but the guy unloads a thunderous uppercut that connects with Elias' jaw. I jerk my head to the side, desperately trying to get out of the way of his big head flying back.

"Watch out!" I scream as the man lunges forward.

Elias grabs him and wraps his big arm around the man's neck. His face is only a few inches away from mine. He's grunting and struggling to get out as Elias holds him.

Do something!

I reach over and slap his cheek as Elias chokes him. His fierce eyes snap open and he growls at me.

Elias doesn't like that at all. He picks the guy up and slams him into the ground, which finally makes me fall off. I land on my ass as Elias pummels the guy with fists and elbows.

"*No*," I gasp when I turn and see the second giant

grizzly bear approaching. He's stalking forward on his big paws with his head lowered, vicious eyes locked on me.

I stand up on my trembling legs as he lifts his head and lets out a deep thunderous roar. Elias is busy beating the other guy to a pulp, so I'm on my own. On my own to stop a freaking grizzly bear!

My hand is clutched around the gun, but I can't shoot another bear!

"Go away!" I scream as I throw the gun as hard as I can. It flies right into his mouth and gets lodged in his throat.

"What happened?" Elias says as he stands up, breathing heavily and looking at me with the sexiest eyes I've ever seen.

The bear is bent over, choking and hacking away as he backs up with wide eyes. Geez, it's almost like I planned that!

"I threw the gun at him! I'm sorry!"

"No! That was great. Let's get out of here."

I jump over the unconscious guy who's splayed out on the ground and follow Elias over to the dirt bike. He gets on and revs the engine.

I've never been on a bike with a motor before. I'm not sure what to do.

"Come here," Elias says when I hesitate for too long. He grabs me and lifts me onto the seat in front of him, only we're stomach to stomach and I'm straddling his big strong body.

I wrap my arms and legs around him, burying my face into his warm chest as he takes off like a rocket. I scream as we fly through the forest.

It's thrilling and adventurous and I'm all kinds of turned on from clinging to this sexy man.

I look at the gash on his shoulder to make sure he's

alright, but it already seems to be healed. There's some dried blood on him, but no more wound. I remember reading somewhere that shifters have enhanced healing powers. I'm just glad he's not hurt.

"That bear was choking," I say as we eventually slow down when it's clear that they're no longer chasing us. "Should we go back and help him?"

"You want to do the Heimlich maneuver on a thousand pound grizzly bear?"

Clearly, I didn't think about the logistics of that. "I guess not."

"Don't worry about him," he says. "I saw him spit it out in the mirror."

He slows the bike to a stop and lets me climb onto the back. I'm a little disappointed as I swing my leg off and let go of him. I liked straddling his big muscular frame. My pussy was grinding against him with every bump and now, I'm so wet that I can feel it with every step.

He looks in the direction we came as I sit behind him and wrap my arms around his big torso. My hands slide right onto his shredded abs. I guess this position is pretty amazing too.

"I think we're good," he says as he starts riding the bike a little slower. "They're not going to come after us. Especially since the man who's paying them is dead."

My palms slide down an inch when we go over a bump and I can't help but think about how close my hands are to his cock. I wonder if he's as turned on as I am right now.

We ride for a while in silence and my mind goes back to that room. Troy had me tied up to the bed and there was no getting away from him. I don't even want to think about what would have happened if Elias hadn't come bursting into the room to save me.

"Thank you for coming for me," I whisper as we ride under the light of the full moon.

He looks at me over his shoulder with a look that makes me breathless. "We're mates, Ava. Living life without you wasn't an option."

I squeeze his body a little tighter. "Are we really mates?"

"Can't you feel it?" he asks in a soft voice. "The yearning? The attraction? The intense feeling of being drawn to each other? I feel it so strongly for you. You're all I want, sweet girl. All I want is you."

I swallow hard, not knowing what to say. I feel the same, but I don't think I'm ready to say it just yet.

"Do you know where we're going?" I ask.

"I know every inch of these forests," he says. "My bear has been roaming through them for decades. If we continue up here, we'll arrive in town."

"Do you think there will be a bathroom I can use?" I ask with a gulp. Now that the danger is over, I have to go really bad. Every bump is killing me.

"I'll find you one," he says as he speeds up. "And then... We'll go back to the auction."

"*Back* to the auction? Are you crazy?"

"I stashed the money that I brought to bid on you nearby in the forest."

"You brought money? To win *me*?"

"I sold my ranch and gave up everything for you," he says like it's nothing.

"You did? Why?"

He suddenly stops the bike and turns to me with a look of pure love.

"I would do anything for you, Ava. *Anything*. I'd give up everything I have just to hold you in my arms. I sold my ranch to make sure I was the highest bidder, but Novak outbid me. Well, he's dead now, the ranch is ours, and we have a bag full of money waiting for us. We can use it to start a new life together."

He's staring at me with his beautiful hazel eyes and it makes my heart turn to mush. All he's done for me... I'll never be able to pay him back for all of it.

I grab his stubbly cheeks and pull his mouth to mine. His big hand slips onto my lower back and he pulls me against him with a hungry moan.

His tongue slides along mine as he claims my mouth. I never imagined that my first kiss would be with a wild man like Elias, but I'm glad that it is. I can't imagine a better kisser than him.

I slide my hands into his hair as he holds me protectively like he's never going to let me go now that he's finally found me.

My head is spinning when we finally pull away. I can't help but smile as I admire his gorgeous face.

He's older than me with a few more wrinkles and salt and pepper hair, but I *like* it. I trace my tingling fingertips over the lines beside his eyes, wishing I was there all those years to see them form.

I may have missed a lot, but we're together now and we're not going to waste any time.

"I still can't believe you're here," he says as he stares at me in awe. "You're so beautiful. Are you even real?"

My eyes drop and my stomach sinks. "In some ways, no." I'm looking better than I ever have thanks to the team of makeup artists and hair stylists that did their magic, turning my ordinary-looking face into a masterpiece. I'm terrified that he's going to be disappointed when he sees how I really look once I wash off all this makeup and take down my hair. "I don't normally wear this much makeup."

He kisses me again and I moan into his mouth. God, he tastes good.

"You'll always be stunning to me, Ava," he whispers after he pulls away and gazes into my lovestruck eyes. "Always."

I wish I could believe him.

We continue driving to the town and by the time we arrive on the dark quiet streets, I'm *dying* to go.

The only thing that's open is an inn.

We hide the bike behind the building in case those bears make the stupid mistake of coming after us and challenging my man again, and we head inside. I have to go so badly that I run in.

"Can I please use your bathroom?" I ask the man at the desk with a wince.

He doesn't even look up from his book. "Bathrooms are for customers only."

"Oh, come on!" I say as I bounce around. "I'd expect this in the city, but I thought people in the country are supposed to be nice!"

"It's not worth arguing over," Elias says as he tosses some bills onto the counter. "We'll take a room."

"Where did you get that?" I ask in shock. The man is shirtless and barefoot, wearing only a pair of exercise shorts. Unless... Did he keep it in—?

"It was in the storage compartment of the bike," he says as the man rings us up and hands over a key.

"Oh," I say with my cheeks blushing as I grab it.

"You're on the second floor," the jerk-head receptionist says. "Second door on the right."

There's an elevator, but I have to go so badly that I race up the stairs and burst into the room.

Elias waits in the hall.

I stop before I slip into the bathroom.

"You can come too," I say to him.

He walks in with a smoldering look in his eyes and slowly closes the door.

Chapter Eight

Ava

"I'm in a hotel room with a man," I whisper as I stare at my shocked face in the mirror.

Of course, being in the same room as a man was always going to be the inevitable conclusion of tonight after being auctioned off, but it's still shocking now that it's happening for real.

I swallow hard as I look at the makeup on my face. It's beautiful, but it's not really me. None of this is. I pull the pins out of my hair and shake it free.

If anything is going to happen here, I want it to happen with the real me, not with this fake persona that I can't possibly keep up.

After my hair is hanging loose, I wash the makeup off my face with water and soap. I wipe my cheeks and eyes with the towel until my familiar face is looking back at me in the mirror.

I hope I'm enough for him...

With a deep breath, I head into the room with my stomach churning and find him sitting on the bed.

He looks up at me and stares in awe, like I'm the most stunning girl he's ever seen. Like I'm even more beautiful than before.

"*Wow*," he whispers under his breath. "You're incredible, Ava. I didn't realize you were so beautiful under all that makeup. I mean..." He closes his eyes and shakes his head like he screwed up. "Not that you weren't beautiful before, it's just... Look at you. Wow."

He keeps staring at me with those gorgeous hazel eyes and I just have to kiss him. I march over, straddle his big body—my torn gown hiking up my thighs—and crush my lips to his, kissing him so hard I practically shove my tongue down his throat.

He doesn't seem to mind in the least. His big arms wrap around me and he holds me tight as he kisses me back.

"I waited for you," he says between kisses. "I'd wait a lifetime for you."

I stop and look into his shimmering eyes as heat blooms inside of my chest. "What do you mean? You've never...?"

He shakes his head as he stares at me.

"With anyone?"

"Never. Not even a kiss."

He's so hot that he could have had any woman he wants. I'm sure there were hundreds of them throwing themselves at him over the years. Maybe even thousands. And he never even touched one? For me?

"I only ever wanted my mate, Ava," he whispers as those possessive hands slide onto my ass. I moan when I feel his strength. "I only ever wanted you. And now that I've finally met you, I know why. You're the most spectacular girl in the world."

"But no other girl? Really?"

He licks his lips and the sexy sight makes me so wet that I squirm on his lap. "I don't think you'll ever know how much I fucking want you, beautiful girl. We're mates. That's all that matters to a bear shifter. It's all that matters to me. You might not feel the connection as strongly right now, but you will. Every day that we're together, our bond will get stronger. And once my mark is on you, you'll start to really understand. There will be no doubt in your mind that you'll be mine forever."

The spot on my neck under my ear begins to tingle. I reach up with a trembling hand and touch it.

"That's right, sweet girl," he says in a low rumbling voice. "That's where my mark will go. Once I sink my teeth into that spot, you'll understand the full power of being a bear shifter's mate."

I swallow hard as I look at his mouth. I want to feel it on me. I want to be his.

"Oh, Elias," I whisper. "I've waited too. I never kissed a man either. I've never done anything. You must think horrible things about me for being in that auction, but I... I don't know. I just felt so compelled to go."

"That was fate," he says as he slides his hand into mine. He traces a circle on my palm. "She was giving us a helping hand. She was bringing us together."

"We're together now..." I whisper as a hungry need begins to take over.

He growls low as those big hands slide back onto my ass. "Yes, we are."

His eyes fall to my parted lips and I shift a little closer to him. We both moan when my pussy lands on his hard cock.

"*Oh shit,*" I moan as he starts rocking my pussy along his throbbing erection by moving me back and forth with his big strong hands. He's gripping my ass cheeks and making me so turned on I feel like I'm going to melt as my aching pussy moves up and down his thick shaft.

Tingles erupt along every inch of my skin as I slide my fingers up the back of his head, threading them through his soft hair.

"*Oh, fuck,*" I moan uncontrollably. "*Oh, Elias...*"

I start bucking and grinding against him, moaning uncontrollably as the pressure and tension inside builds to a crescendo. I can't stop moving my hips. I can't stop feeling that hard dick on my pussy. The force is unbearable. The intensity overwhelming.

"Cum on me," he growls in my ear and I shiver against him. "It's okay, baby. Let it go. I want to feel it."

The tightness inside builds and builds as I move faster and faster, unable to stop myself. "Yes!" I scream as I grab a fistful of his hair. "Fuck yes!"

The tight squeeze inside me contracts one last time and then releases, drowning me in intense pleasure as I cling to this beautiful man for support. I scream out as tears stream down my cheeks and waves of heat crash through me. It's so intense. It's so good.

I whimper and moan as I continue rocking against him while the first orgasm of my life flows through me.

"That's my girl," he says as he rubs my back with a satisfied smile on his face.

"I'm sorry," I say, blushing in embarrassment as I squeeze my eyes closed. "I didn't mean to... you know, so fast. I was trying to hold myself back."

"Never hold yourself back with me, Ava," he says with a

fierce look in his eyes. "*Never*. I want all of you, unbridled and unrestrained. Never hold back."

"Okay," I promise as he leans forward and presses his mouth to mine.

The last remnants of the orgasm are glowing through me as he claims my mouth.

Those big hands slide up my back and he pulls down the zipper on my dress. It comes loose around my body and something in me snaps. I want it off. I want it all off.

I yank off the straps and he does the rest, pulling my pink gown down as he kisses my chest. I'm wearing a strapless bra and he makes quick work of it, pulling it down before I can even unclasp it.

My breasts tumble free and I watch with my pussy aching as he lunges on them, sucking the hard nipple on one while massaging the other with his big strong hand.

I drop my head back in bliss as he rolls his tongue on my nipple, teasing, taunting, and caressing it. His mouth is so warm. It feels so good. He switches to the other breast with a groan and I wonder if he can hear how hard my heart is pounding.

I'm aching all over for him. I just had an orgasm but I want another one. I want to feel him inside me. I want to do every single dirty thing he's been waiting to do to me for decades.

I unclasp my bra and throw it across the room as he coats my hard nipples with his tongue.

Those big manly hands suddenly pick me up and he lays me down on the bed.

I look up at the sexy sight of him with my pulse racing and my pussy aching. He grabs my dress and pulls it down my body, his heated eyes blazing with every inch of skin that comes into view.

This man is so erotic. So sexy. I feel my heart twisting at the sight of him standing over me with those intense brown eyes locked on my body.

He pulls the dress down my legs and off my feet and a tingling rush of adrenaline tingles through me. I've never been so exposed for a man, but I like it. I want him to see all of me.

My eyes roam to his thick shoulders and onto his big muscular arms. I lick my lips as I admire his massive chest and shredded stomach.

His cock is enormous and stiff as concrete as it presses against the inside of his shorts.

"Did you find something you like?" he asks with a deep growl in his voice. I lick my lips and nod my head as I stare at it, wondering how it can be so big. "Do you want to see it?"

My eyes snap up to his and I can barely breathe as I nod. "Yes."

He grins as he pulls down his shorts and that big throbbing cock springs out. It looks even bigger, longer, and thicker in the flesh.

"You see what you do to me?" he growls. "You see how fucking hard you make me?"

I'm throbbing all over. My hands are aching to touch him.

"You're my mate, beautiful girl," he says as he wraps his hand around it and starts stroking that thick firm shaft. "You say the word and it's yours. Now, until the day that I die, you can do whatever you want with it."

My body reacts in a strong way, craving it fiercely like I've never craved anything before.

He suddenly lets it go, but it still stands straight up. I'm mesmerized as I stare at his thick veined shaft with his beautiful masculine balls hanging below. They look so full. They look so ready to unload.

"You'll feel it in you soon," he growls as he leans forward and grabs the waistband of my panties. "You'll feel every thick inch deep inside you, I promise."

I suck in a breath and lift my hips as he pulls my panties down. He takes them off in one smooth motion, pulling them off my feet and letting them drop onto my dress.

"That's it," he says with a heated look. "Open those legs for me. Show your mate your pretty little pussy."

An erotic rush spreads through me as I open my legs, letting him see it all.

He swallows hard as he stares at my pussy, the first man to ever see it. I've kept it safe all these years and now it belongs to him.

"*Fuck*," he growls as he drops to his knees and grabs my thighs. I whimper as he yanks me closer.

My heart is pounding as I watch him lower his head between my legs until his face is only an inch away. He inhales deep and his whole body shivers.

"All mine," he growls possessively as he stares at my soaked virgin pussy. "It's mine now."

My head nods all on its own as the spot that's destined for his mark tingles like crazy. "It's yours, Elias."

He looks up at me one last time and then dives in, devouring my pussy with his hungry mouth. My back arches and a scream rips out of my throat when I feel his hot tongue plunging into me. It's so *deep*. It's so *good*.

His mouth moves everywhere, coating every inch of me as I grab the sheets on either side of my head. I feel like I'm falling. It feels like I'm spinning out of control.

Those big strong hands are planted on the inside of my thighs, keeping my legs spread wide apart as he hungrily pushes his tongue into my virgin hole. With the way his big shoulders are moving and with the grunts and growls rumbling out of his chest, it looks like he's enjoying this experience even more than I am, but I know that's impossible. Elias is giving me the most intense sensations I've ever felt.

Any doubt that we're not mates vanishes as my hips writhe and roll to the rhythm of his tongue.

He knows just how to touch me.

He knows just what to do.

I know now... My body was fucking made for him.

Chapter Nine

Elias

I can't get enough of this juicy little cunt. My girl is moaning and writhing on the bed as I eat her pussy out like I'm never going to stop.

I slide my tongue up her wet slit, tasting every single inch of her before tracing my tongue around her clit and sucking on it hard. Her hips buck as I latch on and suck relentlessly.

"Do you like that?" I ask with a growl as she grabs her gorgeous tits and squeezes them. "Do you like my hot tongue on your little virgin kitty?"

"Don't stop," she moans in ecstasy. "*Please* don't stop."

I grin as I dive back in, moving my tongue down to her tight entrance. She's sopping wet and each lick I give her tastes as sweet as warm honey.

I touch her soft pussy lips with my fingers and then slide one of them into her tight little hole. This pussy is virgin tight and I keep thinking it's going to loosen up from my hot tongue, but it's as tight as ever. She's clenched around my finger and squeezing like she doesn't want me to leave.

I'm going to breed this girl. There are so many things I want to do to her. I want her bred, I want her claimed, I want her marked so that every man in the world will know she belongs to me.

With all of these hungry urges ripping through me, I latch back onto her clit and suck it hard until she cums all over my mouth.

The orgasm erupts inside her and she screams so loud that I'd be surprised if half the town didn't just wake up. I wrap my arms around her thighs, hold her to my mouth, and let her hot pussy juice leak onto my tongue.

"That's my girl," I moan as I get up with my cock aching. We're watching each other with lust-filled eyes as I wipe my mouth with the back of my hand. "You taste so good, baby. As sweet as sugar."

I let my ravenous eyes roam over her naked body as she trembles on the bed, the last waves of her orgasm crashing into her and making her whimper.

I'm the only one who's seen her like this. I'm the only one who's tasted that sweetness.

My Kodiak bear grumbles inside as I look at her exposed neck. He wants our mark on her. He won't leave me alone until it's planted on her flesh.

That's enough, I growl at him after he snarls in my ear.

He snaps back and charges to the surface. I flex every muscle in my body and grunt as I struggle to push him back down. The force sends me stumbling back into the dresser.

Enough! I roar. *We're claiming her body. The mark is going to have to wait.*

My cranky fucking bear doesn't like that answer. He snarls and charges to the surface again.

I flex my arms and chest tight, and push him back down with a growl. He gnashes his teeth at me and paces, getting ready to do it again.

My heart is pounding as I squeeze my eyes shut, bracing myself for a charge from the beast.

I feel my mate's gentle hands and soft mouth instead.

My bear retreats with a grumble as I slowly open my eyes to find Ava on her knees in front of me with her lips wrapped around my cock.

I moan as she squeezes the base of my dick with her tiny hand and starts to take me deeper into her mouth.

She looks at me with those big lusty blue eyes as she drags her flat tongue up the base of my shaft. A bead of pre-cum oozes out of my head as she gets close to the top. With a sexy moan, she takes me back in and drinks it down.

"Oh god," I moan as my body relaxes and my muscles go slack. "That sweet little mouth... You feel so good, baby."

This is a sight I'm going to remember forever—my beautiful virgin mate sucking my hard dick for the first time... Fuck, she's incredible. I can't get enough of her.

She gently cups my balls that have been filling up for her all night as she forces me into her mouth as far as my cock will go. That big load she's holding in her hand is destined for her womb. I won't unload into her mouth no matter how badly I want to. Not tonight anyway.

Tonight, I have breeding on my mind.

"You're amazing, Ava," I moan as I slide my hand into her silky brown hair, threading my fingers through it as she pleasures me. "I'm in love with that sexy little mouth."

She moans in delight as she coats every inch of my dick

with her tongue. How can she be so good at this already? How can it feel so amazing?

When I feel the pulse of an orgasm about to erupt through me, I realize that I have to stop her. It's torture, but I do it.

"There's only one thing I want more than to cum in that hot little mouth of yours," I say as I slide my hand along her jaw. I gently pull her chin up until my cock slides out of her mouth. "And that's to cum deep in your virgin pussy."

She wipes her wet lips as she looks up at me with glossy blue eyes.

"On the bed, my love," I say in a throaty voice as my anticipation and need build to a feverish pitch. "Spread those legs for your man."

She gets up and does what I say, strutting to the bed and then laying down on it. I moan as I grab my wet cock and watch her spread her legs for me.

That beautiful pink pussy is glistening with her virgin juice. I can't wait to take that cherry. I've been waiting thirty years for it.

The moment is finally here...

The anticipation is killing me as I walk over to the bed while stroking my wet cock.

"You ready for it?" I ask as I climb onto the mattress with the lustful smell of her cunt tingling in my nostrils and nearly driving me mad. "You ready to be claimed by your mate?"

"Do whatever you want to me, Elias," she says as she wraps her legs around me and pulls me onto her. "I'm your mate. I'm your girl. I can handle it all."

She pulls my mouth to hers and I kiss her hard as my cock lands on her spread pussy. It's so warm and inviting. I shiver at the thought of sliding into her and feeling her virgin warmth wrapped around me.

"I'm glad it's you," I say as I grab my cock and slide my thick head to her opening. "I'm so happy you're my mate."

"So am I, Elias. I've never been happier."

We kiss one more time and then I push my swollen head inside her.

She rips her mouth away from mine and cries out when I push in another thick inch. Drops of perspiration appear on her chest. I drag my tongue between her breasts, licking them up as I slowly drive in deeper.

"*Shit*," she winces with her eyes squeezed shut. "You're so big, Elias. You're so *fucking* big."

I don't want to hurt her, but this has to be done. I have to stretch this tight little cunt out so we can have fun every day. It won't always be like this. Just this first time.

"It's okay, baby," I whisper as I kiss her neck. "You're doing so well. Just another few inches."

I push my hips forward, driving my cock in deeper until I arrive at some resistance. I grin, knowing it's her intact cherry. It's got my fucking name on it.

I kiss the spot on her neck that's destined for my mark and then thrust through her cherry with a firm pump of my hips.

Her back arches and she cries out as I slide deeper inside. This tight little pussy squeezes me like it's trying to make me pay for defiling it. Like it's trying to choke my cock to death.

The wetness... The warmth... The tight squeeze... I've never felt pleasure like this. She's fucking perfect.

The base of my cock hits her clit and she lets out a deep moan when she's taken in every thick inch I have.

Neither of us can talk. Our foreheads are touching,

mouths open, as we stare into each other's eyes. We're finally connected. We're finally one.

"That's my good girl," I whisper on her lips. "Taking every thick inch of your man."

She squeezes her eyes shut and whimpers as I rock my hips.

"You're doing so well, baby," I whisper as I start to pull back. "Don't forget to breathe. It won't hurt for long. I promise."

She exhales long and hard, and then takes another deep breath as my cock slides out of her cunt. I glance down at my shaft and groan when I see her pink virgin cream all over me. I'm coated in her. It's a beautiful sight.

I grab the base and slide it back inside, a little harder, a little faster. Her cunt takes me in easier this time, but she still arches her back and stiffens with a whine.

My girl is tough and takes every thrust I give her. It's not long before some of that intense grip loosens and she begins to take me in easier.

"*Oh yeah*," she moans as she gets into it, rolling her hips as I slide in and out.

She's the sexiest thing in the world with her brown hair spread all around her and her big beautiful tits heaving with every breath. She bites her bottom lip and moans when my hard pelvis hits her engorged clit.

"How does it feel?" I ask with a growl. "Getting fucked by your mate?"

"You feel like heaven," she moans as she digs her fingertips into my arms. "I *love* your big cock. Never take it away, *please*."

I grab her hip and tilt her up, driving forward and thrusting even deeper inside her.

She's clinging to me like she never wants me to leave her little pussy.

My Kodiak growls inside, getting impatient for more. He has his eye on her neck and he's not letting the desire to mark her go.

Enough, I warn as he snarls in my ear.

I'm not letting him ruin this. This is the best moment of my life.

He lunges forward, giving me his own warning as he nearly breaks through before pulling back at the last second.

My vision goes black and I grit my teeth as I hold him down with a growl.

"What is it?" Ava asks.

I open my eyes to find her gazing up at me with her hand on my cheek.

"Nothing," I grunt as my hips move back and forth in a faster rhythm.

"We're mates, Elias," she says as she looks at me with pure acceptance and love. "Tell me. Please."

"It's the mark," I say, hating that my bear is ruining this. "He wants me to mark you."

She touches the spot under her ear and her mouth opens as her eyes flash with excitement. "Do it."

My bear grumbles like he's saying 'I told you so.'

I'm thrusting my hard cock in and out of her tight little cunt as she pleads with her big blue eyes. "I want to be your mate in every way," she says with a moan. "I want to feel it."

My sweet girl turns her head to the side, exposing her long slender neck. My mouth waters as I look at the spot.

The urge becomes unbearable. I feel my body swelling up as I fixate on her flesh. She cries out as my cock gets thicker and longer inside her, stretching her virgin cunt out even more.

I want to apologize. I want to tell her this is a bad idea. That she's been through enough.

But the animal side of me is taking over and I can't stop staring at her neck.

My gums ache and then burn as my canines grow long and sharp. I pull back my lips with my heart pounding in my chest.

I fuck her harder and faster as my arms, chest, and shoulders swell. I must look like a monster, but my girl looks more turned on than ever.

"Do it, Elias," she begs. "Mark me. Mark your girl."

I lunge forward with a possessive growl and sink my teeth into her soft sweet flesh. She screams and digs her nails into my skin as my mark takes hold.

I can feel her becoming mine. There's no going back.

She bucks and convulses as I hold my teeth in her skin, and it takes me a second to realize she's cumming. Her hot little pussy erupts on my cock and coats me in her warm cream.

Finally, once the mark is complete, I slide my sharp canines out and my body returns to normal.

She's still writhing in the blissful pleasure of her orgasm as my arms and chest shrink back to their usual size.

"Holy fuck, Elias," she moans when she finally opens her eyes and looks at me. "I see what you meant now. I can feel it. I'm yours, baby. I'm all fucking yours."

Our mouths connect and I kiss her like never before. She's finally all mine. All fucking mine.

"Turn around," I growl when I finally pull away.

She cries out in agony when I pull my cock out of her. This angel of mine quickly jumps up to her hands and knees as I posture up behind her with my wet creamy cock in my hand.

"That's it," I say as I slowly slide it back in. Her whole body erupts in shivers at the feel of me penetrating her in a new position. "How does that feel?"

Her head drops. "So fucking good," she moans.

I grab an ass cheek in each hand and squeeze hard as I begin to thrust in and out of her cunt.

I'm trying to be soft and gentle, but it's impossible. Breeding this beauty is back on my mind it's all I can think of.

Control slips out of my grasp and I fuck her harder, thrusting into her like I'm punishing her pussy.

She cries out every time I slam into her. The headboard smacks the wall with every drive of my hips.

"I'm going to cum," I growl when I feel it building inside.

My balls are aching they're so full. With every thrust, they smack into my girl's clit and send her closer to the edge.

All I'm thinking of is filling that sweet ripe little womb with my hot load as I drive in deep.

I want her bred. I want my girl to be carrying my bear cub.

With a fierce roar, I squeeze her ass, lodge my hard cock inside her, and cum *deep* in her pussy.

She cries out as her pussy orgasms for the forth time tonight while taking every drop of my seed.

My cock surges and surges, hot cum shooting out with each jerk of my shaft inside her.

I will my seed to find its way to her womb. I won't leave this pussy alone until this sweet angel is carrying my child.

She takes it all and then collapses onto the bed with a groan.

I sit on my heels with a deep breath, watching as she closes her eyes and immediately falls asleep.

She's so perfect.

She's here.

And she's mine.

Chapter Ten

Ava

"That's the last of them," Elias says as we watch from the mountainside while the last two trucks pack up and leave. All of the private jets are gone, the billionaires heading off around the world with their new virgin brides, and the huge tent has been put away. "We can go now."

We start walking down the mountain as the last two trucks drive out of the valley and pull onto the road.

It's over. It's finally over.

Elias smiles at me and my whole chest warms up.

The rest of our life together is finally beginning.

It's still dark out with dawn on the way and the light of the full moon is lighting up our path as we casually walk down to the valley. I smile as I look up at all of the gorgeous stars in the sky, shining like a thousand diamonds over our heads. I'll never get used to this stunning view.

"It's so beautiful out here," I say as I admire the dark silhouette of the trees on the night sky. "I love the mountains and forests. They're spectacular."

"You're going to love my ranch," he says as he takes my hand and tenderly holds it. "It's more beautiful than this."

"Really? How's that possible?"

"You'll see," he says with a grin. "We have lakes, rivers, stunning mountains, and rocky cliffs. My bear loves roaming through the wilderness on our property. The house is beautiful too. I hope you'll like it, but I think you will."

"I'm sure I will," I say shyly. Any house with this man living in it is one that I'll love.

I guess this means I'm staying?

I really don't want to go back. I want to have a life with mountains and forests and rivers and hot sex. I want a life with this man who gets me going like no one else can.

He stops and turns to me. "So, that means you'll stay? With me?"

I shrug shyly. "If you'll have me."

"Of course." He wraps his big arms around me in a warm loving hug. I close my eyes as I'm engulfed by this perfect man.

I swallow hard as something that's been bothering me comes into my mind. I don't want him to think badly of me. I want to start off right.

"You know, Elias," I say with my cheeks blushing. "I didn't want to marry that man. I—"

"You don't have to explain, Ava," he says with a loving look in his eyes. "Sometimes we do crazy things for love. Sometimes fate drives us to weird places before getting us where we need to go. I'm just so happy you're here. I'm so relieved. You know what you're like?"

"What?" I ask, smiling uncontrollably.

"You're like a Christmas gift that you wanted every day for thirty years and then you get it, and it's even better than you thought it would be."

I step on my toes and kiss his chin as my eyes water. "That's the sweetest thing anyone has ever said to me. Maybe, I'll let you unwrap me later."

"It's Christmas all over again," he says with a flirty look.

I laugh as we continue walking down the mountain and into the valley.

"What do you do for Christmas?" I ask him.

"It's always so fun," he says with a big smile. "All of my family comes for the day and I make a huge feast. Turkey and the works. But don't worry, I'll do everything. You can sit back and relax the whole time."

That sounds amazing. I spent the last five Christmases reading a book in a Chinese restaurant by myself.

"But we can miss it this year if you want us to see your family instead," he quickly says. He's so sweet.

"I don't really have any family, Elias. The last time I saw them was when they were on the news. And it wasn't the good kind of news. I have family. But they're not *family*."

He nods, knowingly.

"You're a part of my family now, Ava. You're not alone anymore."

I've been alone for so long. It feels good to have someone to rely on. Someone to care for me.

"I can't wait for them to meet you," he says with a smile. "You're going to love them and they're going to love you. Like me, they've been waiting a long time to meet you too."

"Oh no, so much pressure! I hope I don't disappoint them."

He shakes his head. "That would be impossible."

"Oh look!" I say as we walk into the middle of the valley. Fireflies begin glowing all around us. It's magical.

I've never seen anything like this. It's beautiful.

Elias catches one in his hands and shows it to me. "Cup your hands," he says. "Hold them together."

He puts the firefly inside and I close my hands.

"Ahhh!" I screech playfully. "I can feel it flying around in there!"

"Keep it in there," he says as he catches another one. "It will be worth it."

He catches a bunch more and keeps stuffing them inside my hands until I can feel my palms buzzing.

"Now, open it," he says softly as he watches.

I lift my hands as I open them and it's like dozens of little sparks of magic flying out.

"That was so cool," I say as we continue walking to the forest.

I'm so curious about him. I want to know everything. I realize that even though I know we belong together, I still haven't learned all the small stuff.

"So, are you like a... stay in kind of guy or go out every night and socialize kind of guy?"

"I like to stay in," he says. "I hope that was the right answer. But if you want to go out, I'll go out with you. I'll do anything with you, Ava. I'm just so happy to be by your side."

"I'm happy too."

We stop and kiss in the valley under the moonlight with the fireflies igniting all around us.

Elias exhales in relief when we find the bag of money where he stashed it.

My mouth drops when he unzips it and I see all the

stacks of crisp one hundred dollar bills. There's so much money in there. Like, *so* much.

"You were going to spend all this?" I say as I stare at it in shock. "On me?"

"I would have given ten times this if I had it," he says in a serious tone. "I would have given anything for you. I would give you my life."

"How much is in here?"

"Seven point five million dollars."

All that... For me. He's crazy.

I like crazy.

I kiss him on the lips and smile as I pull away. "I have good news. You can have me for free!"

"Then, we'll spend the money on an amazing life together," he says with a nod.

I almost forgot...

"I'm rich too! I have a million dollars to add to the pile."

"Then we have all the money we need," he says as he gazes into my eyes, "and all the love we need. It looks like our future is going to be just—"

"Perfect."

He nods as we smile at each other. "Perfect indeed."

Epilogue

Ava

Two months later...

"Be brave, little buddy," I whisper as I pat down the soft earth around the baby tree. "You got this. I'll come visit you when you're as tall as my man over there."

"Are you talking to the trees again?" Elias asks with a grin.

"No," I say as I hurry over to him.

He gives me a look as he grabs another tiny tree from the huge bag slung over his shoulder.

"Okay, maybe a little. Just a few words of encouragement, that's all."

He leans forward, gives me a delicious kiss on the lips, and then scoops out a chunk of dirt with his shovel, drops the tree inside the hole, and gently pats it down. He does it all in one smooth motion, moving so fast it's a blur. Meanwhile, I take forever with each one. For every one tree I plant, he plants about ten.

Every little bit helps though. We're replanting all of the forest that Troy Novak and his company clear cut. It's been a huge project—and we're not even a third of the way done—but it's been very rewarding and spending time with Elias is always a joy. He's so fun to be around.

I love looking at the side of the mountain and seeing all of these tiny trees taking root. I can't wait to come back here in twenty years and hike through the forest that my man and I planted.

Elias keeps going, planting tree after tree as I sit on a larger boulder and take a quick break. He's so sexy. I love watching him.

Those big arms flex and tighten with each stroke of his shovel. He wipes the sweat off his brow with his thick forearm and I have to fan myself as I watch.

I love that he's older too. Older men are so sexy. How did I not realize that before? He's forty-five and I'm twenty-five, but that twenty year age difference makes no difference to us at all.

He knows how to treat me right and we always have the best time together. We really are meant to be.

I wanted some excitement and adventure in my life, and with Elias, I definitely got it.

He finishes off the trees in his giant bag and then walks over to the pile of other bags and slings another one over his big shoulder as I watch.

It's late November with a chill in the air, but he's only wearing a tank top and those big sexy arms are all jacked from the physical labor.

"Are you naming them again?" he asks with a smile as he walks past me.

"Am I that obvious?"

His smile widens and I can't help but smile back. He points to a little baby tree beside a rock. "Who's that?"

"Marvin."

"And that?"

"Penelope."

He grins as he drops the bag and comes over.

My heart races as he drops to a knee in front of me and places his big strong hands on my stomach, cradling it.

"Penelope," he says as he stares at my belly that's not showing at all yet. "I like that. We should put it on the list if it's a girl."

He leans down and tenderly kisses my stomach.

"But what will the tree think if we steal her name?" I ask with a grin.

He laughs as he shakes his head. "Can we name the tree something else? How about Rebecca?"

"Fine," I say with a deep exhale. "But Penelope, I mean Rebecca, is not going to like it."

He kisses my stomach once again and looks up at me with those big beautiful eyes. "I'm so happy we're together, Ava. And I'm so happy you're having my child."

I cup his cheeks and pull his mouth up to mine. He kisses me softly and gently until my body is ready for more. "I'm happy too, Elias. More than I ever thought was possible."

We kiss again as the sun shines down and the birds sing all around us. They're scoping out the new trees, but they'll have to wait a few years before they can move in again.

I can't believe my luck.

I came so close to letting this all pass me by. If I hadn't

built up the nerve to dial that number and take a chance, none of this would have happened. I'd still be bored out of my mind in the library right now, instead of in the arms of my dream man in the most spectacular place on the planet with a baby growing in my womb.

Sometimes you have to take a chance in life and I'm glad that I did.

I wouldn't have been living this adventure without it.

"I love you," Elias says as he kisses my forehead. "And I'm so excited for our baby to arrive."

I smile, happier than ever. "I love you too. I'm so excited for it all."

Epilogue

Elias

Twenty years later...

"Isn't it so magical out here?" Ava says as we walk around the forest. I love the adorable smile she always gets whenever we walk around here.

We each have an arm linked around our oldest child, Penelope. Our other three children are up ahead in their bear forms, exploring the mountainside as we enjoy the last weekend before Penelope goes off to college.

I'm trying not tear up. God, the years go by so fast. It felt like yesterday that I was cradling this amazing child while she was in her mother's womb. I still remember the amazing feeling at seeing her for the first time. Ava was so strong throughout the delivery. I fell even in deeper in love that day. For the first time, we were more than mates. We were a family.

"Dad, are you crying?" Penelope asks as she looks at me.

"No," I say as I quickly wipe my face. "I think a bug flew into my eye."

"You are crying," Ava says as she scrunches her face up like she does whenever she sees a new kitten or a puppy.

"Stop," I say with an embarrassed laugh. "I just... I can't believe you're leaving."

Penelope kisses me on the cheek and then squeezes my arm. "I'll be back at Thanksgiving *and* at Christmas."

"And the whole summer, right?" I ask with an eyebrow raised.

She nods like the good little girl she is. "Definitely! We'll hang out the entire time. I promise."

"Penelope!" our youngest, Mitchel, shouts from up ahead. "Our Kodiaks are going swimming in the lake!"

She smiles at us as she wiggles out of our grip. I don't want to let her go, but I have to.

"I'll catch you guys later."

I turn away as she quickly gets undressed and phases into her Kodiak bear. Ava gathers up her clothes and puts it in the backpack I'm holding as I watch the bear who was once my little cub hurry after her brothers and sisters.

"I can't believe she's leaving," Ava says as she puts her head on my bicep and watches her go.

"I know. I feel like my heart is breaking."

"Just think," she says as she looks up at me with a flirty look. "Once all the kids are gone, it will be just the two of us again."

I grin as I look down at her. "I'm listening..."

She slides her hand into mine as we walk. "We can have naked Thursdays and have loud crazy sex all over the house whenever we want."

"Now you're talking," I say with a grin. "How long until the others move out?"

"Probably about seven years…"

"That's too long," I joke. "I'll call a boarding school when we get home."

"Now you're talking."

We both laugh and smile as we continue walking up the ridge. We get to the top, surrounded by the gorgeous forest that we planted with our own bare hands, and look down at our four Kodiak cubs playing in the lake.

Ava and I look at each other and we just know. We don't even have to say the words.

We're so proud of the family we built and so grateful for the life we have.

I squeeze her hand as she rests her head on my bicep and moans contently while we watch our kids splashing around and having a blast in the water.

I'm so thankful for my Ava.

Without that crazy auction, I might never have found her.

And that would be a life I wouldn't want to live.

The End!

Read all NINE books in the *Highest Bidder* series:

Available on Amazon!

Come and join my private Facebook Group!

Become an OTT Lover!

www.facebook.com/groups/OTTLovers

Become Obsessed with OTT

Sign up to my mailing list for all the latest OTT news and get a free book that you can't find anywhere else!

OBSESSED
By Olivia T. Turner
A Mailing List Exclusive!

When I look out my office window and see her in the next building, I know I have to have her.

I buy the whole damn company she works for just to be near her.

She's going to be in my office working under me.

Under, over, sideways—we're going to be working together in *every* position.

This young innocent girl is going to find out that I work my employees *hard*.

And that her new rich CEO is already beyond *obsessed* with her.

This dominant and powerful CEO will have you begging for overtime! Is it just me or is there nothing better than a hot muscular alpha in a suit and tie!

All my books are SAFE with zero cheating and a guaranteed sweet HEA. Enjoy!

Go to www.OliviaTTurner.com to get your free ebook of Obsessed

Also by Olivia T. Turner

More complete shifter series are available now!

The Ridge Brothers

Get them on Amazon (in Kindle Unlimited)

Alphas in Heat

THE ALPHA'S OBSESSION

Carnal ALPHA | Dirty ALPHA | Feral ALPHA | Forbidden ALPHA

kindleunlimited

The Dixon Brothers

ALPHA Possessed | ALPHA Consumed | ALPHA Dominated | ALPHA Unhinged

kindleunlimited

FERAL SHIFTER UNTAMED | FERAL SHIFTER UNSTOPPABLE | FERAL SHIFTER UNLEASHED | FERAL SHIFTER UNHINGED

NASTY RABID BEASTS

Come Follow Me...

www.OliviaTTurner.com

- facebook.com/OliviaTTurnerAuthor
- instagram.com/authoroliviatturner
- goodreads.com/OliviaTTurner
- amazon.com/author/oliviatturner
- bookbub.com/authors/olivia-t-turner